Our Little Aztec Cousin of Long Ago

This edition published 2026
by Living Book Press

ISBN: 978-1-76183-132-4 (hardcover)
         978-1-76183-131-7 (softcover)

First published in 1934.

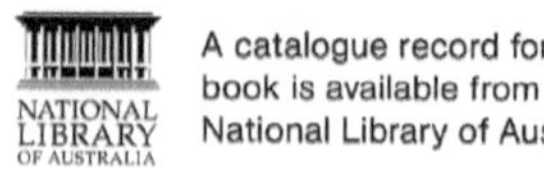

Our Little Aztec Cousin of Long Ago

by

Elizabeth Borton

"His Thoughts Were Elsewhere"

Contents

CHAPTER I

A Boy at School

Coyotl sat on a straw mat in front of his teacher and practiced writing. But even as he mixed the paints before him in little shallow bowls of earthenware, and dipped his brush in the color, his thoughts were elsewhere.

He and the other students, all boys of about his own age, were writing on leaves of paper made of the pressed pulp of the maguey bush. They were practicing the simplified drawings which the Aztecs used for writing. Rabbits, leaves of corn, bundles of reeds, a man seated—all these pictures meant words, as written in different combinations—to the Aztecs. Writing by means of pictures which everyone understands, as we all understand letters, is called hieroglyphic, or picture, writing.

There was no use hurrying, or wishing to be through with the lessons, and gone, because in the Aztec schools the boys lived with the priests, in a special building inside the great pyramid—temple or church, and they were not allowed to return to their parents again for many years—until all their schooling had been completed.

The priests of the temples were wise men, and they had much to teach their pupils.

The priests of the Aztecs, besides administering services and sacrifices to their Gods, and devotion by means of eternal fires, and prayers, were students of the stars that revolved overhead in the black night. They knew arithmetic, and the sciences that tell about the earth, and animals, and plants. They knew the history of the Aztec nation, and they knew its system of government, and the rules of manners by which a good citizen should conduct himself.

All these things they taught the boys entrusted to their care in the temple schools. They also taught them the feast days, and the days made sacred to certain divinities, for the Aztecs had many Gods. And they instructed their pupils in how to make offerings of flowers and fruits at the altars, and how to feed the sacred fires at other altars, so that at no time would the Gods be neglected or made angry by lack of devotion.

Coyotl had been in the school five years. He had entered the school when he was six, a small, slender, brown-skinned boy, with dark intelligent eyes under his smooth black eyebrows, and a thick lock of purply-black hair that fell down over his forehead.

It was in his seventh year that his father and mother and little sister had died in a plague. He had no one now. Probably he would some day become a priest himself. He did not know. And yet, though he was devoted to his Gods, especially to Quetzalcoatl, the Feathered Serpent, who was the God of flowers and agriculture, and of water and the air, he did not want to be a priest. Adventure called to him. He longed to be free to roam the country over, to explore the great city of Mexico which lay outside the temple walls, and which he could see only from the great altar of the main temple where the sacred fire burned night and day.

The schoolroom where Coyotl sat was made of heavy stones, of a gray color, with an occasional stone of a pinkish-cream mixed in with the others. The stone floor was covered with a reed mat, on which were painted designs with a brilliant red paint that Coyotl knew was made by crushing the bodies of little insects. The ceiling of the room was made of wood and stone, and all the wooden beams were richly carved. Light streamed in through a window behind where the teacher sat on a cushion stuffed with bird's feathers.

The teacher, who was droning instructions to the boys, rocking comfortably to and fro as he sat, was wearing a dress of cotton cloth on which a design had been painted in purple dyes, and in his black hair he had twined a purple cord.

The boys wore white cotton garments, and simple sandals made of leather on their bare feet.

Coyotl heard the droning voice giving instructions. The teacher was calling out a list of words,—a kind of dictation—which the pupils were expected to write on their leaves of paper.

But Coyotl was dreaming of other things.

He was remembering the history lesson, and wishing that he had lived back in those adventurous days before the Aztecs had settled down into cities and established schools. He would have liked to be a soldier with the great army of the Emperor of the Aztecs, on that day when Mexico City was founded in the midst of the swampy land between the high mountains.

"It was after conquests and much traveling," the history teacher had told them, "that the armies of the Emperor came to a wide land of lakes and rivers. The mountains rose into the sky all around them like the edges of a bowl, and at their tips the fog clung in white steamy clouds.

"At the borders of a lake, suddenly the Emperor stopped and held up his hand. All were silent, for everyone saw what he saw. Sitting on the limb of a prickly pear tree was a great royal eagle, bearing in his talons a writhing serpent. The eagle sat with spread wings, ready for flight, and his outstretched wings were against the glow of the rising sun.

"The omen was so auspicious that the Emperor then and there gave offerings and prayers, and decided to found a city, to end his people's wanderings, and there to live."

Thinking of this, Coyotl started sketching—not what the teacher directed him to do,—but the form of a great black eagle, with out-stretched wings, and in his claws, a snake.

He was so absorbed in what he was thinking, and

in the drawing he was making, that he did not notice the ominous calm which had fallen over the class. The teacher had raised his eyes, and had noticed that Coyotl was not paying attention.

While the boy continued his drawing, oblivious, the teacher got up off his cushion, and came to where Coyotl sat with his paints and leaves of paper. He was putting a glow of gold behind the black wings of the eagle—a glow to represent the rising sun.

"You have been wasting my time and yours," said the teacher quietly and Coyotl was so startled that his nervous hand spilled a little dish of ink. The purple liquid crept slowly along the reeds of the mat. And Coyotl felt his heart beating fast inside him, because the discipline at the school was strict indeed, and he knew that he would not be easily pardoned.

The teacher turned to the other pupils, who looked at Coyotl with sympathetic eyes, but could not say a word to help or encourage him, for that would have been against rules.

"You will go to your rooms," said the teacher, and the boys began hastily gathering up their inks and paper. They tiptoed from the room, and Coyotl looked up at the teacher with miserable apologetic eyes.

"Go to your room now," said the teacher, "and in a little while I will come to you, and I will tell you what discipline I have decided to give you."

Coyotl picked up his things with trembling fingers. It had seemed a harmless enough thing to do, but he knew the rules. And the punishment was strict. If a boy in the priests' school broke discipline, he might even be sentenced to death, or sold into slavery. Montezuma, the great Emperor, wanted his subjects to be obedient, and the teaching began young.

Coyotl's room was a tiny cell, painted white inside, with a small window opening into one of the courts. He had there a bed of reeds, and a low bench made of wood, and on hooks in the wall hung his other cotton clothes.

He went to his room and sat down disconsolately. There was no one he could talk to; no one to whom he could whisper that "he hadn't meant any harm—he was only imagining…"

A little before the sun went down, the teacher came to see him in his room. Coyotl immediately rose to his feet and offered the teacher his seat. Then, with hanging head, he awaited his sentence.

It didn't come at once, and the boy glanced at the teacher's face inquiringly. The teacher was looking at him kindly.

"I am not going to punish you, Coyotl," said the teacher. "You are a bright boy, and your drawing of the eagle was good. But I cannot let you fall into these habits of dreaming. You must stay up with me and tend the sacred fires, and pray until the morning. It is not your turn to watch the fires again so soon. You will be sleepy. This is your punishment.

"I will await you at the great fire on top of the main temple as soon as the first stars appear. Do not be late. You must be washed and clean, and wearing your sacrificial robes."

"I will be ready and I will not be late. And thank you," breathed Coyotl.

The teacher did not say another word, but as he left the little room, he dropped his hand forgivingly on the boy's dark head, and let it linger there a moment.

CHAPTER II

Rules are not Made to be Broken

Coyotl put on his robes of pure white, with a border of red—the same red dye in which the whole robe of the teacher-priest had been dipped. Through his little window, Coyotl could see the first stars shining in the still light-blue sky, where the pink clouds of sunset were drifting. It was time to go. The fires at the altars were heaped high at night, and burned brightly, so that the people, unsafe and insecure without their God the sun looking down at him, would at least have the protection of light from fire. The god of fire, Quetzalcoatl, would protect them.

Coyotl went out through a central hall onto a balcony that ran around the entire square building like a porch, and led toward a set of stairs which ascended the building to another similar balcony. This in turn led to another stairway, which ascended to the flat top of the great square pyramid. On this flat summit a fire burned night and day.

From that summit of the pyramid Coyotl could see over the whole city, which was lighted almost as brightly as at mid-day by the fires of this temple and of others, and by the sacred fires which burned on the top of all the walls which surrounded the city. Out beyond those walls, lay the roads leading into remote sections of Anahuac. And out there—beyond the city, into the night, into adventure, the boy's thoughts wandered.

Coyotl knelt in front of the fire, and made his prayers and offerings of flowers and perfumed woods which sent out sweet fragrance as they burned.

The night was coming down quickly, black, but spangled with stars. Through his cotton robes Coyotl felt the chill winds that rose with the darkness, and the sacred fires reached out and leaned toward the south, as the wind grew stronger.

Piled round about the small altar in which the fire was made, were the woods, cut in sections, which tradition said were to be laid on the flames in a special sequence, in order to please the gods. Beside them stood golden jars in which oils, blessed and spiced, were kept, for the oils facilitated the burning in bad weather. Bad weather or good, the fires must be kept up.

There was a sound of drums and singing from one of the lower balconies, and Coyotl knew that a procession of youths from the school, with their priest-teachers, was forming for the nightly parade of obeisance to the sacred fires. One of the youths was chosen every night to help tend the fires and watch them and pray until the morning, in company with a priest. This night, Coyotl was to watch the fires again, even though but two nights ago this had been his duty. Already the lack of sleep burned against his hot eyelids.

Closer and closer came the sound of the boys' voices, and the deep throbbing notes of the drum. Now they were ascending the last stairway, and now they were walking toward Coyotl.

The priest was robed in a dress of cotton, dyed brilliant red, and there were feathers and flowers in the golden headdress that sat upon his forehead like a crown. His arms were full of flowers, and his expression was one of grave and tender devotion. The boys followed behind, singing.

The rites were simple, slow, and performed with meticulous care. Then began Coyotl's long watch through the night, which he was expected to punctuate with prayers and devotions. Twice he would be visited by a priest during the night, once at midnight, and once when the first morning stars began to shine.

Coyotl knelt and said his prayers when he was alone again.

Then the watch began. The stars crawled across the sky as the hours went by. Night sounds from the street came up to his ears—a parrot screaming, calls, and the night barking of dogs.

Coyotl's eyes drooped with weariness; he longed for his little room, and his bed of rushes spread with a cloth. But there was still most of the night before him. The stars had not yet wheeled into that place in the sky which would tell him that it was near midnight.

He was not supposed to, but the hours were so long that he went to the edge of the top of the pyramid and looked down into the street. There was a man passing by; across his back he had a big bundle, and at his heels followed a dog.

"How wonderful," thought Coyotl, "to be free

to go, to leave the city, to take a bundle on your back and walk out, into the night, bound for some far place!"

It was then that he heard a tiny sound—a heart-breakingly pitiful sound. He looked about for it. It was a sort of chirp, like that of a little hurt bird. He could not find anything, and yet those little cries continued.

By listening carefully, he thought he could detect where the little cheeps were coming from. From the balcony below.

Coyotl was torn between desire to go straight down and find out what was making those sounds, and the knowledge that he must stay and watch the fires. To neglect them was a crime; to let them die down meant to involve the city and the whole nation in disaster and destruction, and to induce the wrath of the gods.

Yet that pitiful cry of some little bird in distress caught at his heart. He decided suddenly.

He walked all around the edge of the pyramid at the top, and looked down. All silent and quiet. No one about.

He banked the fire, and put on two pieces of wood.

It wasn't proper to do it so, but Coyotl heard again those plaintive cries for help.

Then, gathering up his robe, he hurried down the stairs and went to look for the poor little bird.

Ah! There it was. A little thing. An eaglet. How could it have come there? It was frightened as he approached, and yet courageous, too, for it tried to hop away, and yet one claw and one wing had been hurt, and they dragged pathetically.

Coyotl put his hands around the bird's trembling body, picked it up and gently examined it. A broken wing, a crushed leg and claw. Oh pitiful! Some one had hurt it. Some child may have hurled a rock at it. Yet, they could be mended, thought Coyotl. Someone could heal the eaglet. He would heal it. How to keep it? How to hide it until the morning, when he would be free to take it to his cell and bind up its wing and wash and bind its claw?

As he pondered, he forgot that time was passing.

Silently, on his leathern sandals, the priest-teacher had ascended the stairs, and now stood near, watching him with disappointment and disdain.

"Coyotl, you have left the fires!"

Coyotl could say nothing, but he held his bird

'*Ah! There It Was!*'

closer. His heart beat as fast and as loud as the little frightened eagle's.

"Come with me."

The priest led him up again, and made him cast the bird aside, and lie down on his face before the fires, to pray the gods for forgiveness.

There Coyotl staid, flat on his face, until the morning, and his heart failed within him, for he knew that the penalty for disobedience such as his was death. Death or slavery, and he did not know which could be worse.

The sun rose, slowly and then suddenly, flooding the valley of Mexico and the lakes nearby with warmth and color. The clouds glowed pink and golden, and the sky flushed, then turned pale green, and finally blue,—a soft satiny blue like a petunia petal.

The sun warm on his back through his cotton robe only told Coyotl that the time of his punishment was at hand.

Silently, the priest led him back to his room. The morning offerings had been given, the morning prayers said. Another priest and student tended the sacred fires. Coyotl sat in his cell thinking sadly that he would never see it again, never again hear the voices of his comrades singing and talking together, never hear the drums that he loved, or look out over the city of Mexico, and long to be part of it, on its streets, within its houses, part of the city's busy life.

He was comforted that the priest had taken the wounded bird in his arm, and had carried it away to be cured. One of the priests was adept at cures, at binding hurts, and making sick people well. He would know how to make the eaglet fit for the blue skies again, free and happy—not earth-bound.

The teacher stood in Coyotl's doorway, a dark figure, shutting out the light. He said no word. His face was stern, his lips set in a severe line, but his eyes were very sad. He said nothing, but Coyotl knew that he was to follow him. He was to go before a conclave of all the teachers. His crime would be told. His punishment would be meted out. He bowed his head, and followed the teacher.

The priests, in their ceremonial robes of red, were meeting in one of the council chambers of the pyramid-temple-school. In the center of the room sat the head priest of the temple, with his feet on a rug made of woven feathers. The feather rug was the only furniture of the room, except the heavy stone benches on which all sat, ranged in a semi-circle.

Coyotl threw himself on his face on the floor to await judgment.

The teacher-priest spoke.

"This lad broke discipline in the classroom. I was dictating. He set down, instead of the words I gave, a drawing of an eagle, clutching in its claws a writhing serpent. His punishment, he knew, should have been more severe than that which I gave. But since his drawing was of the eagle, a good omen, I made the punishment that he watch the fires again last night, though he had watched them before only two nights ago. At midnight I ascended to pray with him, but I found him on the balcony below. Yet, again, in his hand was the eagle of good omen—a wounded small bird which I have taken to the doctor priest for care. But he had left the fire untended."

The head priest considered.

"The punishment is death," he said quietly, and an involuntary shiver passed through the body of the boy as he lay on the stone floor.

"But because the omen may have meaning— because the eagle was with him each time—I will give him into slavery. But he must be sold to a good master. Because of the omen, he should not be killed, either as punishment, or by a cruel owner.

"To the first good man who comes to this temple to make offering after noon today, shall the boy be given in slavery, to do with as he will, but not to be killed."

The audience was ended.

The priests rose and left the room, silently.

Coyotl remained on his face, on the floor.

But after all the others had left, the teacher-priest raised him to his feet, and supported him on his arm back to his cell. He said nothing, but his eyes were kind and pitying.

Somehow, as he lay down to sleep, Coyotl felt comforted. The eagles may have been a good omen, really! Perhaps the god Quetzalcoatl had heard his prayers to wander in the world, to see and learn and do. Perhaps this was his means of releasing him, an orphan, who might otherwise remain in the temples forever. And thinking so, smiling, he fell asleep.

CHAPTER III

Uncle Amotl, the Merchant

Merchants were much honored by the emperor Montezuma. Traveling about through the kingdom, with a number of armed men in their party to carry and protect the merchandise they had for sale, they formed powerful small bands that often proved to be valuable in emergencies. Then too, the merchants could report to Montezuma, when they came back from a long trip, on the welfare of provinces in which they had travelled and whether or not certain wealthy nobles had paid all their taxes. Also, Montezuma often called upon a traveling merchant to act as his ambassador or messenger, carrying gifts and letters of greeting to some subordinate sovereign or noble.

Amotl, the merchant, had taken leave of Montezuma, and was busy preparing himself for a trip to the furthest edges of the great kingdom of Anahuac.

He was now a man of nearly sixty. His hair was still black as a bird's wing on his large head, but his craggy, dignified features were seamed with wrinkles, and his black eyes had a look of peaceful understanding that seems very often to come into men's eyes as years go by.

In his youth he had always been on the road, with his burden-bearers following him, each man armed, and loaded with about sixty pounds of merchandise.

But of late years, he went less often, seldom more than once a year, and usually it was at the request of his sovereign, though there were very few people in the kingdom who knew how much Montezuma valued the wisdom and prudence of Amotl.

Uncle Amotl (trusted friends of Montezuma were "Uncle," as a title symbolic of esteem) was about to depart from Mexico City for the north, and he was not very happy about going, because danger threatened.

Pacing up and down restlessly in a small room in his beautiful palace on the hills of Chapultepec, inside the City of Mexico, Montezuma had confessed to Amotl that he distrusted the loyalty of certain nobles of the ally-state of Tezcuco, but that he wished to be assured that they were plotting against him before he sent his armies to force them into submission. "And

I have heard of thieves in the mountains," he said. Thieving was punishable by death.

The room to which Montezuma had summoned Amotl was small, but it gave upon a garden that was carpeted thickly with flowers. Hangings made of the down of birds woven into cloth, and intricately dyed in a beautiful pattern alternated upon the walls with hangings made of colored bird's feathers sewed upon cotton in a lovely design. A small richly carved seat of wood, with inlay of pearls and gold, was the only furniture of the small room. That seat was for Montezuma alone.

"I must war against those nobles if they plot to evade the payment of taxes and men that they agreed upon," said Montezuma, "because if the states to the south learn that we have lost Tezcuco as our ally, they will rise against us. You must take out a train of men, with rich stuffs, and go into the homes of the nobles in Tezcuco, and report to me, by special messenger if need be, the state of their loyalties and their strength. You will start as soon as you can arrange your party." Amotl had little trouble in gathering together rich merchandise likely to tempt the wealthy nobles into entertaining him and his followers for some days.

The nobles, many of them, lived on vast estates in the country, growing corn and vegetables, and raising fowl and animals for food. Though their homes were luxurious, and they had many slaves and employed workers, their lives were likely to lack the excitement afforded by the great cities of the capitol, and the visit of a merchant laden with precious goods, was an event of great importance and excitement for all members of the household, especially the ladies.

Amotl would gather his loveliest jewelry of gold bracelets; earrings made like wheels to be inserted in the ears; linked necklaces, with turquoise beads set in gold; finger rings made to be worn near the nail, with a long piece of gold designed to cover the nail completely; little nose ornaments in the shape of a small round peg to be worn through that part of the nose which separates the two nostrils from each other, just above the upper lip. And he would pack also jewelry made of white jade, and strings of pearls, and ornaments of all kinds made of tortoise shell.

Then he would make special packs of the most beautiful of fine feather weaving,—robes, rugs, and wall hangings.

For the ladies, besides jewelry, he might take an

assortment of finely woven veils of fiber, some of them sewn with precious stones, toilet articles made of tortoise shell, and many other trinkets.

Amotl had not made a long, wearisome, and hazardous journey for some time, and his old heart almost failed him at what he was to undertake. He would much have preferred simply fitting out some younger merchant with the goods to sell, and resting behind quietly among the spicily fragrant flowers of his gardens. But Montezuma's wish was a command.

Therefore, arraying himself in clean robes, combing his hair with sweet-smelling oil, and taking offerings of his choicest and loveliest flowers, and of gold and pearls, he betook himself to the temple-pyramid in the center of the city, at mid-day, and made ready to pray and to ask for safe-keeping and success on the journey.

Through the busy market square in the center of the city, Amotl walked, the sun shining on his freshly-oiled hair, and drawing fragrance from the flowers in his arms. In the square there were sections set aside for each sort of special article on sale—foodstuffs, especially corn meal, pepper powder, chocolate, potatoes, squashes, fowls and fishes. And cloths. And flowers, for those too poor to own plots of ground where they might raise their own. Jars and pottery for dishes. Everything you can imagine that was needed for life and comfort, the people brought together in the great central square every fifth day, and traded, or sold for set prices. And there were special overseers or magistrates, wandering among the booths and stalls to see that everything was done with justice and with no confusion.

Amotl passed by one booth where a house-wife was purchasing her week's supply of chocolate, for which she paid with the Aztec money—little pieces of tin cut into a shape like the letter T of a standard size, thickness, and shape. This chocolate she would later mix with vanilla, with the sugar from corn stalks, and with spices to make it into a sweet frothy drink which the Aztecs used as a beverage with meals, and as a dessert.

At another booth a feather-weaver had just sold one of his loveliest hangings to a noble, who was paying for it with a currency of higher value than the tin money—transparent quills, filled with a set weight of gold dust.

A steady stream of merry, musical people, men

women and children, was flowing through the square. Some emerged from the temple. Others went in. Even though it was mid-day the flames from the sacred fire at the altar on top of the pyramid shone for some distance, and Amotl raised his eyes reverently toward that swaying tribute to the gods.

He entered the temple just as the beams of the sun fell directly below on the sun dial which told the priests that it was mid-day. Amotl advanced through the cool dusk of the courts toward the inner altar, and there he laid down his flowers and jewels as an offering, and prostrated himself on the stone floor to pray.

He felt a touch on his shoulder. It was one of the priests of the temple. The priest signed to Amotl to follow him into one of the inner chambers.

There they remained for some time. But within the hour Amotl emerged from the chamber, and following him, with bowed head, was Coyotl, a slave boy.

Out through the pyramid courts, and into the bright sunshine of the day they went, and Amotl silently began the walk to his home.

Coyotl, behind him, stepped along swiftly to keep

up with Amotl, because when Amotl was unusually thoughtful or busy with some problem, he walked faster than many young men.

Though his head was bowed, as he became a slave, Coyotl's heart beat with happiness. He was to live in the great city at last! In his soul he gave thanks to Quetzalcoatl.

"Thank thee, God of sunshine and living things! Thank thee! For thou hast granted my wish! I walk in the streets of Mexico!"

CHAPTER IV

Amotl's Home

The streets of Mexico City were lined on either side with flat-roofed houses, and over those roofs ran a profusion of brilliantly colored flowers, the sweetness of which came drifting past the nostrils as little occasional breezes stirred the air.

Most of the houses were made of a sort of porous red stone, cut into thick square pieces. The houses were built simply, with square doors and windows, and they rambled over a good deal of territory. Here and there Coyotl and Amotl passed clusters of reed huts, plastered together and made safe against the wind by mud which had been put on damp, and then allowed to dry in the sun.

Some of the streets were broad and fair, and paved. These were the principal thoroughfares. Most of them were somewhat narrow, and unpaved. But the city as a whole was clean, and the abundance of water from the neighboring lakes, some of which was carried through the city by means of well-constructed canals, made it possible for every houses to have its little garden bright with flowers. Some of the people who had more land than the others grew fruit trees and vegetables for their food as well.

Amotl walked swiftly and thoughtfully through the streets to his home. He had not planned this year to take slaves. He had no need for another slave for his household. Yet the gods had bestowed on him this boy. What was he to do with him?

"Well," he thought, "all I can do is take him with my train, as far as Azeapozalco, and sell him in the slave market there. But the slaves brought to that market are usually accomplished, able to sing and dance, or perform special household duties. This boy cannot. And I cannot let him go into slavery for manual labor in the fields. He is too young. I shall have to talk with him."

So thinking, Amotl, who did not wish to go on the long wearisome journey through Anahuac and the neighboring states anyhow, sighed deeply, and bowed his head.

Coyotl, walking meekly behind him, saw the sight and wondered about it. But he could not be unhappy long. It was such fun to be out walking along those streets, with houses on either side, in which he heard merry sounds of talking and singing and laughter. It was all so interesting to him, who had been so long inside the temple courts and rooms—the honeysuckle bunching down over the pink houses, the men walking past him, some of them poor and barefooted and carrying heavy burdens, and some rich, walking easily and freely, with their square cotton cloaks floating out behind them.

Now and then a litter would come down the street,—a sort of seat carried on poles which were hung across the shoulders of two men. Inside there might be a noblewoman, her hair covered by a fine gauze veil, held in place by a wreath of flowers. Or a noble, with his black hair covered by a helmet made of metal, into which were stuck many precious bright plumes and feathers.

A group of the soldiers of Montezuma, were marching in orderly array down one of the streets. Each man wore a quilted cotton vest, light and not too warm, yet capable of turning aside arrows. Around their loins they wore girdles of cotton cloth, and on their legs gaiters made of the quilted cotton.

Their heads were protected by metal helmets, and each man carried, stuck into his girdle, daggers with sharp edges made of flint, and an arrow quiver. On his left arm he carried a shield made of leather, and his bow. Nearly everyone had a staff which was made of heavy wood, with tiny sharp pieces of flint inserted into the wood at regular intervals, making it into a sort of combination saw and club.

But the walk, interesting though it was, did not last more than about forty minutes. Amotl lived in a section of the city where the trees and ferns grew thick, where there were still many little crystalline streams gushing through the gardens, and where there were as many canals as streets. In their swift light canoes, the people moved along the canals, bound on their business, and some of the houses faced on them, and had little landing stations.

Into a house made of alternate blocks of creamy and of rose-colored stones, Amotl turned. There was a wall as high as a man around the house, but the gate was open, and over it hung purple and red flowers. Amotl stopped to sniff the fragrance of these before he kindly motioned to the boy to follow him inside, and Coyotl's heart beat with happiness to see the fair

There Were As Many Canals As Streets.

garden and lovely house in which he supposed he was to live.

Most of the garden consisted of small square patches of earth divided by carefully placed stones, and all the paths were paved. In some of these patches of earth grew every lovely flower that would grow there, and in others fruit trees and shade trees and blossoming trees. The air was heavy with sweetness from the flowers. And in the center of the garden was a square lined pool, full of water, in which fish were swimming.

They entered the house. A white-clad servant brought a bowl of water and a cotton cloth. Amotl gravely dipped his hands in the water, washed them and his face, and then dried them on the towel. After he had finished, Coyotl was given the water, which he poured over his hands. Then he shook them dry, and followed Amotl into the house. There were a succession of rooms, square, with windows open, nicely furnished with carved cedar-wood benches and little tables. Great sticks of wood, oiled at the top and charred, showed from whence came the light by which the inhabitants of the house saw at night. Clean reed mats on the floor made the stone floors less cold, and supplied a decorative note, for they were beautifully painted with designs of birds and snakes and images of gods. Hanging against the walls were tapestries of dyed cotton or weavings made of the feathers and down from birds.

They passed through the rooms of the front section of the house, through an open court, into the back part of the house, which bordered one of the canals. Here Coyotl saw many servants, men and women, dressed simply, with their hair nicely combed but unornamented.

As Amotl came into the court, a tall man of about forty, dressed in a simple white girdle and a blue cloak of cotton, came forward and made a sign of greeting.

"My boy," said Amotl, turning to Coyotl, "this is the keeper of my house. His name is Camana. Since my wife died, and my daughters have been married, we live here like old parrots in a large cage. He will show you your duties, and where you may sleep. I will speak to you once more in the evening. Camana, this boy is Coyotl, from the temple school. He broke discipline, and today he was bestowed upon me as a slave."

Camana bowed, and said, "Follow me."

Amotl turned away into the inner house, and Coyotl followed Camana across the court into a small room, bare of mats, but furnished with a comfortable bed of reeds.

"Rest," said he. "I will bring you some food, and then you may sleep. I can see that you need both."

And indeed Coyotl was so sleepy from his ordeals and his anxiety that he could scarcely hold his eyes open long enough to eat the hot stew of meat and squash that Camana brought him. And when he had left his bowl clean and polished, he lay back on the reeds, and almost at once fell into slumber.

The Journey Begins by Night

It was two nights after Coyotl had been brought to the home of Amotl. Those two days had passed swiftly for the boy. He was up before dawn, washing the stone walks of the garden and the stone floors of the house, and the street in front of Amotl's house, for Montezuma was severe in his laws about a seemly order and care of the streets of the city.

He had his breakfast after morning offerings at sun-up, for Amotl was regular in his prayers and devoted to his gods.

Then Coyotl's duties included caring for the mats and the hangings in the house, doing errands in the town for Camana and Amotl, and any other odd job such as carrying water to certain precious plants in the garden.

Coyotl had found everything he did interesting and worth while. His back and arms were strong for such labor as was asked, for the boys in the temple schools had always been expected to do their bit about cleaning and caring for their quarters and for the halls and rooms of the temple.

"What is the business of my master?" he had asked Camana curiously one afternoon, while he was mending a broken place in the pavement of one of the walks with mud mixed with gravel.

Camana answered, "He is a merchant."

"Does that mean that he keeps a booth in the market place?"

"No indeed. Amotl takes a train of many armed men, loaded with fine goods, and travels far into the country, selling his wares in the homes of nobles. He is no market-place man."

"Ah, how I would like to go with him!"

Camana looked at the boy interestedly. He seemed to be a strong, lively lad, with an alert face, and bright eyes, and he was certainly not afraid of work. He seemed to tackle each new small task with delight.

"Who knows? Perhaps you may go with him," mused Camana. "He soon starts on the most important journey of his life, taking with him a hundred carriers, and he will go to the farthest border of the kingdom and will cross over into the land of the

Tezcucans, who are allies of Montezuma. Maybe Amotl will have need of you."

"Oh, I pray that he may have. I will ask him if I may not go."

"I advise you not to. He is a kind master, but does not like requests or commands from his slaves."

Coyotl was downcast.

"I forgot I was a slave," he whispered.

But as the afternoon slipped by and the round sun descended lower across the blue sky, he took courage. It could do no harm to ask. He did not think he might be beaten. He might be left behind, but then—also he might remind Amotl of his presence. He had not even seen him, except fleetingly, since the first day he had slept in this rose and cream-colored house.

After the sun had set, and Amotl's emptied dinner dishes were carried to the back quarters to be washed, Coyotl took his courage in his hands and approached the master.

It was dark now. Stars shone above the garden. In the rooms of the house Camana had lighted the oil-dipped staffs of wood, and their burning gave out light.

Amotl was resting on a couch, as Coyotl came to the door and looked in.

"Who is it?" asked Amotl without moving and without lifting his hand from across his eyes.

"It is your young slave, Coyotl."

"What do you want?"

"I beg that you take me with you on your journey. I am strong. I can help. I can carry a big load. I can count and watch that nothing is stolen. I can…" This poured out breathlessly, but Amotl raised his hand for silence. His heavy gold bracelets and nail protectors glinted in the light of the fire from the torch.

"I shall take you, and you are to help. But in Azcapozaloc I shall sell you. I have no need for a young slave."

Coyotl crept away silently then. He felt sore and empty inside. His disappointment was bitter. He went to sleep heavy with unhappiness, but in the morning, as he saw the first shadows cast by the house and garden in the thin sun-light following dawn, his spirits rose again. Anything might happen! Perhaps Amotl didn't mean it. Maybe he could make himself so useful that Amotl wouldn't want to sell him!

As he sat over his breakfast bowl, the house and

gardens paths being still wet and shiny from his ministrations, he heard the tramp of many feet outside. Camana went to open the side gate, which was made of cedar-wood, and slung on leather thongs between the high rose-colored walls. Outside there were many men, all wearing strong heavy-soled sandals, and slung across their backs, over their quilted cotton robes, were empty woven baskets. The sun glinted on the daggers in their girdles.

"Come," called Camana to Coyotl. "Make haste and take these men to Amotl. They are to form the train. Today the goods will be counted and packed, and tonight they take the road with Amotl."

And Coyotl's heart beat fast with excitement. Now the great storerooms in back were to be opened! He would see the treasures within! He would be with the others when they left Mexico City that night! He would walk outside the walls of the city!

Amotl was ready. From a chain around his waist, he took out a great key, and he gravely unlocked the door of the storeroom. He made a sign to Coyotl to follow him.

Cedar-wood chests stood against the walls, each

HE MADE A SIGN FOR COYOTL TO FOLLOW HIM.

labeled. Amotl stood a moment in his storeroom hesitating. Then he looked inquiring at Coyotl.

"You can count, can't you?" he half asked, half commanded."

"Yes, master!"

"And you can write?"

"Oh yes!"

Amotl turned to Camana.

"Bring paper-cloth and ink and brushes. We will let the boy keep the tallies."

The tallies were not hard to keep, for Coyotl knew his figures well. Dots represented each number up to five, and after that, up to ten, the dots combined to make the numbers—such as five dots and then two, for seven, and so on. The numbers ten and fifteen each had a separate name, and these numbers were combined with the dots up to twenty to form higher numbers. Twenty was represented by a flag. Larger sums could be indicated by the number of flags and dots written in combination. Twenty twenties was written as a plume. And four hundred plumes was written by drawing a sack or purse. The number writing was really a great deal like Roman numerals. But if only a third of four hundred was supposed to be written, the person figuring might simply draw a third of a plume, and so on.

So, all through the day, Amotl opened his boxes, and drew out treasures to tempt the taste of noble men and women. He tested each piece in his experienced fingers, and then set it aside to be made into a package and weighed by Camana. Coyotl wrote down the article, its weight, the number of the pack into which it was made, and the name of the man who was to bear it on the journey. At nightfall they were finished. The accounts had been made. Each man had his pack, besides the men whose packs consisted of food for the others on the journey.

Amotl was weary, but he did not leave the storeroom until he had looked over the last of Coyotl's accounts very carefully.

"Very well done," he said at last. "You were quick, too." He gave the boy a pat on the shoulder, and Coyotl glowed with pride.

It was night when all was ready, and the men stood, two by two, outside the house, waiting for the signal to start.

"Aren't you afraid some of them might run away?" asked Coyotl of Amotl, and before he knew it, Amotl answered as frankly as if the lad were not his slave, "No. Each man has told his name to a magistrate, and no one will be paid until the journey is over."

The signal was given. Amotl took his seat in a litter, and two men, whose duty it was only to carry the merchant himself, shouldered it. The march began.

All Mexico City was lighted by the fires from torches in gardens and along the streets, and by the sacred fires which blazed on the top of the great pyramid altars. The train took its way straight along through the heart of the city, out the great wide avenue where Montezuma rode in pomp to his wars.

They came to a bridge, manned by soldiers, and Amotl had to present his special permission from Montezuma to cross it. But then at last the bridge was crossed, and they were outside the city walls, walking along a raised road that went straight as an arrow through swampy land.

Coyotl heard the creak, creak of the men's sandals and the soft sound of dust slapped up by their feet. From the swamp came sounds of frogs and insects. The sky was black above, and the light of the torches carried by every tenth man flashed fitfully along the dark road. A wind was rising, and their cotton cloaks blew out from their bodies.

After two hour's tramp the road came down into dry plain, and the dark bulk of little rising hills could be seen ahead. A little prairie fox, the coyote, in deference to the sagacity of which Coyotl's parents had named him, howled.

In another hour the party came to the estate of a friend of Amotl's, whose huge house, with storerooms and gardens and courts to spare, was at their disposal. This was a country home, not so fine as Amotl's, but comfortable. Beds had been made for all the men, and a hot supper awaited them. Amotl ate with his friends inside the house. Coyotl feasted with the men.

"This is splendid!" he said. "I'm not tired at all!"

"Wait until tomorrow," laughed one of them. "You'll feel your muscles! And we'll march farther, too."

But Coyotl went to sleep well content.

"Azcapozalco is still a long way off," he thought.

CHAPTER VI

The Market at Azcapozalco

The warnings of the men began to tell on Coyotl the next day. His back, arms, and legs were very weary as the merchant's train saw in the distance along the road the green gardens and pink walls of Azcapozalco. The sun was hot and it was midday. Down his back, under his cotton robe, Coyotl felt a drip of perspiration, and little beads stood out along his upper lip.

Coyotl walked more slowly. Little by little he fell behind, as they marched. He dropped behind the front ranks that walked in front of Amotl's litter. Then for a time, he walked alongside Amotl's litter, inside which the old man lay on one elbow smoking.

Then, as the sun reached midday, he was near the end of the line.

The men were talking among themselves.

"I hear that we will pitch camp here and rest. The

Uncle Amotl wishes to attend the slave markets. He can't want to buy. It must be to sell."

Coyotl's throat stiffened, and he felt unbearably sad. It couldn't be! It couldn't be that this—even though it was hot and wearisome—was to end so soon.

But before they entered the city, the front ranks of the line stopped, and so, of course, did all the rest of the line then. Amotl was considering. He puffed and swallowed the smoke from his pipe quickly. Then he sent someone to bring Coyotl to him.

"We come now to Azcapozalco," he said to the boy, looking at him gravely. "I have planned to offer you for sale there in the market. What can you do?"

Coyotl pleaded with his eyes, but he answered quickly and brightly.

"I am strong to carry a pack, as you see. And I can figure and write. My calculations are accurate. I would be a good boy for some other merchant, since you do not like me."

Amotl smiled a little, secretly, inside his eyes, but Coyotl saw it.

"I doubt if there will be merchants there," he said. "Most of those who come to buy slaves want them for household entertainers, or servants."

Coyotl answered proudly.

"I am of good family, and even though I did wrong at the temple school, I do not deserve to dance and sing to entertain banqueters, or to live out my life as a house servant's boy."

Amotl was silent and thoughtful. He considered Coyotl gravely. Then he lay back on the feather-stuffed cushions in his litter, and gave the order for the march to continue. Silently, Coyotl let the whole train pass by him, and then began to trudge along behind it. His heart and brain burned with resentment at what was coming, and he felt hurt that Amotl should refuse to see what a good merchant's helper he would make.

The party entered the city and began weaving its way down the quiet streets, past simple stone houses and gardens. It took only about fifteen minutes to come within the sound of business, music, singing and clapping. Punctuating the music there were shouts, as of bids, and Coyotl felt himself freezing with anger and resentment.

They came into the square. There were crowds filling the square so full that it was difficult to pass. The front men in Amotl's line had to shout for passage-way for every step that they took. Out in the center of the market-square, on a raised platform, a little boy of ten, dressed in brightly-dyed cotton, with colored cords woven into his hair, was singing and playing the drum. The bids were spirited. The child seemed to enjoy what he was doing, and at each bid that was higher his eyes flashed and his white teeth showed with pleasure, that he was so much admired.

But! Coyotl did not understand. Amotl's train was not stopping in the square. Slowly but surely they were passing through it and beyond. He was not going to stop! He was not going to sell Coyotl now!

When they had passed through the city on the other side, and were bound out for the plain again, Coyotl relaxed. The evil hour was past. With new energy he gathered his breath for a run, and then he sprinted until he came abreast of Amotl's litter.

"Thank you!" he said, and Amotl turned and smiled at him kindly, and dropped his hand across his shoulder. So they walked on, the old man in the litter, and the proud boy beside him breathing freely for the moment, for he knew that he would not be sold until they returned. And that might be months away.

CHAPTER VII

The King's Messenger

Many days later Coyotl felt as if he had been on the road for ever. The years in the quiet, echoing halls of the temple school among the silent priests were as if they had never been. Even those few days in the flowery courtyards of Amotl's home were like a dream to him.

But the hours of tramping along the dusty roads, talking infrequently with the burden-bearers whose words grew less as the day grew later, seemed now to comprise his entire life. Not having been used to walking long distances every day, the strain on his muscles began to tell upon him, and it seemed as if he must ask them to stop and wait for him.

"I just can't go on," he thought to himself. "I almost wish he had sold me at the market. And this will last for months. I would give my sandals for a drink of water."

As if in answer to his thought, the whole cavalcade

came to an abrupt halt, and the men began murmuring among themselves:

"What's the matter? What's the matter?" Up and down the line there came an uneasy stream of questions.

"Is it time for chocolate?" asked Coyotl hopefully.

"It can't be. We never halt the morning march until midday," replied one of the burden-bearers, whose packs consisted of caked chocolate, one of the chief articles of food on the march. "Can't you tell by the shadows what time of day it is?"

But before Coyotl could answer, one of the leaders of the march came running back swiftly down the road toward where Coyotl stood at the end of the line. His coat streamed behind him, and his feet beat up a cloud of dust as high as his knees.

"The water carrier! The water carrier!" he shouted. "Come at once. The King's courier is dying of snakebite!"

Excitement seized every man in the train. Two of the men whose burden consisted of the water bags, always carried because the cavalcade never could definitely count on streams or springs along the way sufficient for all, ran forward, and Coyotl, forgetting all his weariness, ran after them toward the scene of the excitement, far ahead. The front of the caravan was out of sight around the slope of a hill.

Panting and burning with thirst himself, Coyotl edged and pushed his way through the men who surrounded Amotl's litter.

Amotl himself was standing over the figure of a strange man who had been laid on the cushions of the litter, and was widening a black, ugly hole in the man's bare brown leg just below the knee.

Amotl's flint-tipped dagger dripped with blood, and after a moment, to Coyotl's surprise, Amotl knelt down and set his lips to the wound, and sucked, spitting out the blood at intervals.

"Let us have the water," he gasped, and immediately some was poured into a shallow cup and offered him. He rinsed his mouth and spat out into the dust. Then, dipping the blade of his knife in fresh water, he again opened the wound.

The man in the litter lay breathing with a rasping sound, his eyes closed. He said nothing, but the occasional, involuntary twitching of his muscles, and the rapidly swelling and darkening leg, were indications enough that he was in pain.

The men standing about murmured with sympathy, and shook their heads discouragedly, as if they had no hope for the man who had been bitten.

"We found him here in the road," some one of them said under his breath to another who stood near Coyotl. "A rattlesnake. He had not stopped. The King's courier may not stop. But here he had fallen."

"What if he dies?" asked another. "What becomes of the King's message?"

"Oh, will he die?" asked Coyotl, and someone answered him, "Who knows? Amotl is trying to suck away the poison, and bring the clean blood, but it may be that we found him too late."

"If he dies," said another voice, "we can only hope that he wakens long enough to tell the message to some one of us, so that we can run with it to the next post house. The King's messages must be carried."

Coyotl suddenly remembered the small buildings they had passed a league behind, when they had come out upon the main highway. Each of those two small stone buildings had been patrolled by soldiers of Montezuma, and in one of them Amotl had rested for a few minutes, and exchanged courtesies and news with the keeper of the garrison. And they had occasionally passed the King's Couriers, running in swift relays with news for the Sovereign.

The man in the litter stirred and sat up suddenly and Amotl ordered his men to stand back. The King's courier looked at his blackened and swollen leg, and touched it with his hand. Then, without a word, suddenly and decisively, he drew out of his girdle a small roll of paper.

"I cannot go on," he said, his voice low and choked with pain. "Someone must take the message. There is war in the North."

He sank back on the litter sweating and writhing. Amotl seized the scroll and thrust it into the hand of the man beside him.

"Throw off your burden and run!" he commanded. "Stop for nothing until you come to the post house. Montezuma was afraid of war. All Anahuac will be fighting."

But before the man could unloosen the leather thongs that held his fifty-pound burden on his back, there came a wild shout from the rear.

"To arms! To arms! We are attacked!"

In a twinkling burdens were hurled on the ground. A cloud of dust rose through which Coyotl could see men dropping behind their packs, drawing out their bows and setting their arrows into them. Hasty commands were shouted. Amotl's voice rose above the others: "Don't waste your arrows! Wait until they are nearer!"

Suddenly Coyotl felt a stunning blow on his shoulder which knocked him to the ground. As he got up slowly he realized that his right arm was numb, and that he could do nothing in the defence.

He looked around for a place to hide, and saw that the man to whom Montezuma's message had been entrusted had also been hit and was lying unconscious on the ground, totally forgotten in the press of the sudden fighting. Instantly deciding to be himself the courier, he snatched the message from the wounded man's hand, and began to creep behind the packs stacked up around the litter looking for a way to make his escape.

He saw a ravine some yards distant, heavily grown with cactus and maguey, through which he hoped to gain the road back to the post house. As he ran toward it the distance seemed endless, and the dust in his nostrils made him gasp. Finally, however, he fell forward on his face in the ravine, expecting when he turned over to find a brigand above him. But as he panted in the dust, the moments went by, and he finally realized that no one had seen him.

By wriggling along on his stomach, he made some progress down the ravine. The shouts of battle were still high as he gathered courage and began, half-crouched, to run. At last he dared to stop and look back. Around the packs still swung a maze of fighting men. He watched them for a moment. Then, suddenly realizing that if he could reach the post house, he could not only deliver the message of the King's courier, as he had planned, but could also summon help, he began to run with all his might as if he had never known the weariness of an hour before. His breath came gasping and sobbing, and his throat hurt. But he stumbled on.

He Fell Forward On His Face.

CHAPTER VIII

The Home of the Rich Noble

Hours later,—almost a day later—Coyotl woke in a fresh bed in a small dark room, and lay there thinking drowsily of all that happened. He could scarcely believe it, except for the arrow wound which throbbed still in his shoulder.

The frightened, terribly long, dusty run—gasping and forcing himself—back along the road they had come. At last, exhausted and thirsty and frantic, he had arrived at the post house, and the soldiers, already worried about where the king's courier might be, had carried him into the small cool room, and had given him water.

"Bandits attacked us—they are fighting—the King's Courier is dead of snakebite—his message was that there is war in the north… Send help…"

He didn't remember what had happened then, except that a sense of darkness and peace and comfort had enveloped him, and he had slept.

They awoke him, some time later, and he learned then that soldiers had been sent in haste along the road, and that Amotl had been rescued, and the marauders driven away. But there were dead to be buried, and Amotl's goods had been strewn along the highway. It had taken time to gather them up, and sort out the merchandise which had not been too badly damaged, and repack it.

While another courier had been dispatched along the road with the message of war for Montezuma, a second had been sent to the home of a rich noble nearby to pray that he take in the weary and wounded merchant and his men, and give them hospitality and protection until they could take the road again.

The noble had sent litters for those who were hurt, and had made them all rest at his home. It was there that Coyotl opened his eyes some twenty-four hours after these anxious moments of running wearily and wretchedly down the road toward the post house.

Coyotl sat up and tried to look around him. It was dark where he lay, but the bright yellow streaks of sunlight glinting in through the cracks, and dancing with motes, told him that it was day outside. After a moment he could see more clearly.

He was in the grain room. Cotton sacks of corn had been heaped about for him, and on them he lay, covered by a quilted robe.

There was nobody else there with him. That frightened him faintly for a moment, until he heard happy voices outside, and remembered that probably they had left him to sleep as long as he wished just because he was a young boy, and had brought the help that saved Amotl.

He moved about luxuriously, and wondered whether or not he should get up and go about in search of food. But he decided to sleep a little longer. Still, the sacks of grain were tightly filled, and could have been more comfortable. He got up and began pulling them about in order to make a better bed. He tugged at one, and then another. Reaching down to grasp a third, hidden somewhat under the others, he was startled to feel something of a definite shape, and hard, among the tiny grains of corn.

He felt it carefully. Undoubtedly a dagger! Startled, he could scarcely believe it. Why conceal a dagger here?

He began to feel carefully among some of the other half-hidden bags of grain, and to move them about. Yes. Filled with weapons,—or so it seemed to Coyotl. His heart failed him. There could be no good reason for this. He might ask Amotl about it. He felt further. A handle! A trap-door! Hidden here, under the grain!

Now he was too wide-awake even to want to lie lazily about. He felt his way toward where the sunlight glinted in, in a squarish pattern. It was a door which swung open, and led up a flight of little steps onto the courtyard floor. Coyotl had been put to sleep in a grain cellar.

As he went up the steps he saw that it was about four o'clock in the afternoon. The men of Amotl's party sat about in the sun lazily. Some were polishing their weapons. Others were smoking. They looked disheveled, but rested, and fairly well content.

The courtyard was wide and pleasant, although it was not paved. There were trees, and some flowers, and instead of a fountain, there were water jars hanging suspended from the trees, their damp sides looking deliciously cool, as indeed the water tasted. Coyotl went immediately to get a drink. He was thinking hard. He decided to keep his council, but to do a little quiet investigating.

He looked about him. The low rooms of the house extended ramblingly over the flat plain a great distance, and he could see many little courts within courts, for the noble had wide lands and many soldiers and servants. As far as the eye could see, new corn waved, and the maguey bushes grew in serried ranks like armies.

He went and sat beside one of Amotl's men, a young fellow, whose burden had been one of the choicest packages of jewels.

"Whose house is this, do you know?" asked Coyotl.

"A noble's. His name is Huitl. I do not like his face."

"When did you see him?"

"He was here in the courtyard, not long ago, asking us how we were faring. Amotl was with him, and I know the merchant well enough to feel that I can tell when he does not like someone, too. I should say that Amotl distrusts Huitl."

"But then we will not be here long, will we?"

"We are to have a great feast tonight. Amotl will attend the banquet of the family and friends, and we will show some of our wares. We may be leaving tomorrow. But if there is war in the north… Who knows? We may be turning back."

"Where did you sleep?"

"Most of us slept out here, in the courtyard. He brought coverings enough for us all, and fed us well, but he does not let us have a roof over us. I do not like that. Hospitality should mean the roof as well as the hot bowl and the pipe of tobacco."

"I slept inside. In the grain room."

"Amotl insisted. Huitl would have left you outside too."

"Where are those who were hurt?"

"In the next court. The women servants are washing their wounds and binding them up."

Coyotl walked across the sunlit earthen court to the well, and through the little gate into the next one. Here was a paved patio, where flowers grew, and a little artificial stream meandered through among the bushes. By this stream knelt a servant woman, with a bowl and cotton cloth. One after the other, the wounded men crouched beside her, as she laid damp cloths over their hurts, and bound them on with fresh dry ones.

Coyotl spoke to one of the men.

"Did we… lose many?" he asked.

"Half as many who started will get home again," said the man whose arm was swollen around the ugly red cut left by an arrow.

The Banquet

Coyotl had determined to find Amotl and tell him of the discovery of the hidden weapons in the grain room, but Amotl was busy all day with Huitl, and the little slave did not dare approach the master while he was being entertained by his host.

And yet, just as the sun set, one of Huitl's slaves came searching for the boy. "Your master commands that you present yourself to him immediately. Come with me," he said.

Coyotl followed the slave out of the unpaved courtyard, and through two others, which were paved with stones and fragrant with flowers, before he came to the guest room where Amotl was preparing himself for the banquet with the noble and his family.

Amotl dismissed the slave and summoned Coyotl inside the room. Amotl's feather robe lay ready to be adjusted across his shoulders, and his fine jewels waited to be clasped around his arms and around his neck.

"Hand me my bracelets," he ordered the boy, and as Coyotl took them from the box and clasped them around Amotl's extended arm, the merchant continued: "You will come to the banquet tonight with me, because I trust your sharp eyes. There is something I want you to do. You are to watch Huitl for any hostile or suspicious move. We are near Tezcucan land, and I do not trust this noble."

At this, the nearest approach either to a compliment or a confidence that Amotl had ever shown him, Coyotl burst out with all his suspicions and discoveries.

The words came stumbling over each other in a hurried whisper.

"Master, I slept in the grain room alone. Why alone, I did not know, but I do now."

Amotl turned on him as if to stop him, but Coyotl rushed on.

"Master, the grain bags are filled with weapons. It was dark but I felt them. I felt them inside the bags on which I lay, and out of curiosity I felt all the others. And master, there are weapons for an army in that grain room! And there may be other things in some of those sacks, too. Also, there was an opening into another cellar, hidden underneath some of those bags, and I do not know why that should be, since who could get in, with the bags covering the door below? And the men say they do not trust this noble; they were talking in the court-yard against him."

Amotl stopped the boy imperiously by covering his mouth with his own hand, and as he did so, Coyotl realized that Huitl himself stood in the doorway, shining in his gold jewelry and in his best robes. If he had heard he gave no sign. Amotl bowed and made the customary greetings.

Then he said, "I have not been well since the attack upon us in the road. May I bring my slave boy into the banquet with me so that he may perform small services for me about which I would not wish to trouble your family or your servants?"

"Certainly," replied Huitl, and his smile was all graciousness, though behind his narrowed eyes there was no expression, "though it would be my pleasure to attend you myself, and also my duty as a host. However, if it suits you best, I will command a place to be made ready immediately for this boy."

Amotl bowed his thanks, but Coyotl's heart beat fast for fear he had been overheard, and that he had exposed his master to danger. However, as soon as Huitl had left the room, Amotl turned to Coyotl and said quietly, "You have done well, my boy. It is my wish that you watch this man carefully and constantly during the banquet for any strange gestures, and that you tell me by a sign if you see one. I suspect him of plots against us and against the King. You have already been of help to me. You will be more. Come now, it is time."

With his head a whirl of thought, but both fearful and happy at his new responsibility, Coyotl helped his master adjust the feather-woven robe and put on his head his gold turban with its feather decorations.

As they started through the courtyard toward the banquet room, slaves were lighting tall torches, which gave a sign that the feast was to last for hours. The hall was scented with perfumed oil which burned in little bowls set in niches in the walls. Flowers were strewn over the floor and from the banquet room, where already they could hear a babble of women's voices, came the mixed odors of incense, spicy fruit, tobacco and roast meats. At the doors of the entrance hall stood servants with large earthen pitchers of water, bowls into which it was poured for each guest to wash himself, and white cotton napkins with which they dried their fingers and faces.

Coyotl followed Amotl's example carefully, except that he did not accept a tortoise shell pipe with its pinch of aromatic tobacco, as did his master. They passed along the rows of white-clad servants, who stood on either side of the long table, until they came to their host, whom they greeted with elaborate courtesy. Huitl stood near the end of the table at the further end of the banquet hall until all his guests had arrived. By the time he gave the signal to be seated, there were thirty persons, men and women, and a few boys and girls no older than Coyotl himself, gathered around the table.

From their dress, Coyotl assumed that those boys and girls were sons and daughters of the noble, and that all the other guests besides Amotl and himself were of Huitl's family. The men all sat at one end of the table, but the women, as was the Aztec custom, sat apart from them at the other end, and did not smoke.

The meal was of the best. The servants passed to and fro in their white robes, replenishing the platters of fruits, the dishes of steaming meats and fish, and all the vegetables, cooked in many ways, and plentifully spiced and seasoned.

At last came the sweets, made of maize flour and sugar, in different shapes, and the steaming foamy chocolate, very sweet and flavored with vanilla.

After the chocolate had been served, the young men and girls rose from their places, thanked Huitl for the feast, and went into the patio, from which shortly came the sound of pipes and drums, and of singing.

Coyotl saw the young men and women dancing, as they gracefully flitted past the wide-open doorway of the banquet room. But he stayed close to Amotl, who was now smoking his pipe luxuriously, compressing his nostrils with the fingers of his left hand, and swallowing the smoke. Huitl also smoked, but less deeply, and his eyes darted about the room with a deadly activity, like a snake's.

The conversation hummed about the table after the pulque mugs had gone round, and each guest had received a brimming portion of the intoxicating drink.

Amotl raised his mug frequently with the others, but he did little more than dip his lips in it, for Coyotl saw that he did not empty his mug, and he waved away the servants who went about refilling all those that were drained.

Suddenly a shout and outcry rose from inside the house near the outer gates. Huitl was on his feet at once, his hand on his dagger. Coyotl had tugged at Amotl's cloak to notice this, but Amotl did not need his warning. His weapon was ready to his hand, too.

There were the frantic sounds of a struggle in the halls. The music stopped, and the dancers, wide-eyed with interest, rushed back into the banquet room.

In a moment Huitl's servants appeared in the doorway, trying to prevent about ten men from entering, but Huitl, seeing them, called out, "Let the men come in who disturb me at my banquet. Who may they be?" He stood up scornfully, but his scorn was wasted, for they were the soldiers of Montezuma, led by one of the king's most trusted men, a general, in his war robes.

"Huitl, you will come with us immediately, and command as many of your men as you can equip with weapons to come with you."

"For what?" Huitl was haughty, but Coyotl saw his hand trembling at his dagger hilt.

"There is war in the north, and Montezuma commands that you join him immediately at Azcapozalco, where he is banding together his forces."

"But I should have received less rude word than this—breaking into my house—disturbing my feast—"

Montezuma's soldiers stood in the doorway, with folded arms. Their sandals were dusty; their breasts heaved quickly for they had been on fast march.

"Montezuma directed me to say to you that only because he has need of you and your men immediately does he affront the pride of his noble, Huitl." The commander bowed deep, but he did not tell his men to rest at ease. Stiffly at attention, with watchful black eyes, they stood near, ready to use force.

"I can equip no more than fifty men," said Huitl. "I have not many acres here, nor many men of the warrior age."

The guests had been silent, but now they began to murmur restlessly and frightenedly. The women rose from their seats at the end of the table, and chatteringly excused themselves, and the pat! pat! of their bare feet as they hurried out of the room sounded to Coyotl's ears like bird's wings flying close to the ground.

Montezuma's general looked Huitl squarely in the eye.

"It is treachery to deny Montezuma men for war, or their equipment," he said. "I must ask you to send for all your men except those who will stay to raise enough corn for your family to eat. And bring out all your equipment."

The banquet broke up in real earnest now. The pale servants whisked away the last vestiges of the feast, and the older men who had drunk several cups of pulque took to puffing their pipes in an effort to clear their heads so that they might know what was going on.

"Follow me into the outer patio," said Huitl, and at a sign from him the servants ran forward into the patio with torches enough to light it as brilliantly as if it were day.

"Call all the men," said Montezuma's general, and he stood with folded arms and a stern face, waiting, while Huitl beat on a drum with a heavy stick an impetuous, angry summons.

Hurriedly they came pouring into the patio, servants, field workers, kitchen slaves… more and more of them. At last there was a great crowd in the patio, standing about with restless feet and anxious faces under the flickering glare of the torches. Coyotl swiftly counted a few more than ninety men.

"There are no others," declared Huitl.

But here Amotl spoke, quietly, but flatly.

"There are others," he said, turning to Montezuma's general. "Some are wounded, and some lie dead in the road, but there are still others."

Huitl turned on Amotl with an angry snarl, and his drawn dagger flashed. But Montezuma's general stopped him.

"What courtesy is this? To a guest, it is an offence. To one of Montezuma's councillors it is treason."

"He a councillor?" Huitl's face fell, and an expression of confused surprise spread over the anger in his convulsed features.

"I am," said Amotl, and before Huitl could stop him, he seized the stick and himself beat on the drums with decisive strokes. The low throbbing sound filled the courtyard, and the many-spreading rooms of the house. Timidly a few other men came into the patio.

One limped. Another had wounds in his chest and shoulder, to judge from his bandages.

"Send for them all," shouted Amotl. "Send for all the bandits and brigands. You are going to war. You will swoop down on merchants along the highway no longer!"

Swiftly Huitl turned and darted away like a snake, but Coyotl saw him go, and his warning shout put the soldiers on guard. Two of them caught Huitl and imprisoned his arms.

"I have a hundred men outside," hissed Montezuma's general, "so do not struggle or call to your men. We have suspected you for some time."

He turned then and spoke to the men in the patio.

"All men here will follow me in the morning. There is war, and Montezuma needs every fighter he can find. Because of the danger and the need for soldiers, I will not report that you attacked the merchant. As for Huitl, he will suffer for his treachery. Arm yourselves, and be ready to march at dawn."

The men in the patio,—those who were wounded and the common servants, and the bandits who had escaped injury—conferred uneasily among themselves. Montezuma's general grew impatient.

A spokesman for Huitl's men stepped forward.

"The master armed us always, before… we started… We do not know where he kept the arms…"

"I tell you there are arms for only fifty," shrieked Huitl, struggling.

Coyotl ran forward then, and tugged at the general's arm.

"I know where he hides the arms for his men, and there are arms for many times a hundred!" he cried.

"Where?" The general laid his hand on the boy's shoulder, and Amotl stepped forward proudly, as the boy continued.

"In the grain room, hidden in the bags of grain. They put me to sleep there…"

"Take my soldiers to the grain room," the general commanded one of Huitl's servants, and a trembling man stepped forward immediately to lead the king's soldiers through the patio and into the room in back where Coyotl had slept.

"Wait," called Coyotl, and then, turning to the general again, he rushed on, "and there is another room, a secret room, the door of which is hidden under the bags of grain. A cellar room. Who knows what is hidden in there?"

The general gave orders that the cellar beneath be explored. Then he said to Amotl, "You have a fine boy here. A relative?"

"He is my slave," said Amotl, and Coyotl's heart sank, for he had again forgotten it.

"He has done well," said the general.

The next few events happened with such rapidity that Coyotl scarcely knew what was happening. The soldiers returned, shouting that there were weapons for an army hidden in the grain room, and that in the secret room below there was much grain that should have been paid in taxes—grain enough to feed the army many days. And treasure… Huitl's lootings over a period of years.

CHAPTER X

Montezuma's Audience

Three days had gone by, and now Coyotl and Amotl and his men were but a day's march away from Azcapozalco where Montezuma was collecting together his army from all parts of the kingdom.

Twice since that evening of the banquet which Huitl had cynically given the man he had robbed, Amotl's company had stayed in or near army garrisons, and there amid the bustle and excitement of preparations for war, the little boy had learned more about his country than he had during many long quiet days in the cool schoolrooms of the temple in Mexico City.

Anahuac was allied by thin ties of promises and mutual benefit, with two strong powers to the north. Now one was in rebellion, and the other likely to follow suit. If they broke away from alliances with Anahuac, the country to the south would turn against Montezuma too, and all the fine scientific, agricultural, and scholarly civilization that had been built up in the years of peace would go down. Captures would be made, and the captives would be carried away in slavery, to labor for another land, or to be sacrificed to the grim gods of war.

Because of the war, the courts had not taken long to hear Amotl's case, and to restore him his goods, as well as a percentage of Huitl's grain, as recompense for the disturbance to him, and to the families of the men who had been killed in the fight on the road.

The court had sat, in a nearby town, and had listened to the evidence for both sides, even though Huitl had escaped Montezuma's soldiers the night of the banquet, after his treason was discovered. His family, according to Aztec custom, sent a representative to the court for him.

The judge, in his feathered robes, had heard the testimony of Amotl and of a representative of Huitl. Coyotl had been asked to tell his story of everything that had happened.

A black line was drawn through his portrait by the magistrate, and Huitl's family wept and buried his clothes, considering him as one already dead. Even the court, held out in the shining sunlight, in midday, had interested the boy. The garrisons, and the soldiers, and the look of their bright cloaks and banners as they marched away to join Montezuma to the south, caught his fancy and stirred his strong natural patriotism.

But now he was sad, for tomorrow they would be in Azcapozalco, and there Amotl had said he would be sold. Sold to some other master, taken who knows where, made to do who knows what unpleasant and dull duties. His heart was heavy as they set out, at dawn, on the last march.

Amotl sat in his litter, silent and tired. He had not wanted to go on this journey in the first place. But Montezuma had commanded. Montezuma had not known how soon the flames of war would appear, red and menacing, behind the smoke he had sniffed when he sent Amotl out toward the north, to search out traitors under cover of selling tortoise-shell and feather-work.

Coyotl trudged behind, among the men. He loved Amotl, but Amotl was severe, and Coyotl knew that he would not be persuaded to change his plan. Coyotl knew he would be sold at Azcapozalco.

"Boy, your sandal...."

One of the men pointed down at Coyotl's feet.

The knots of his sandal thongs had come undone, and had fallen behind, somewhere on the road. His sandal flapped uncomfortably, and then came off altogether.

"I shall have to go barefoot," said Coyotl, and unconsciously he flinched a little, for the road stretched long and hot ahead under the glaring blue sky.

"What is this?" Amotl leaned out of his litter, and looked back at them.

"It is my sandal," said Coyotl. "The thongs wore through, and I have lost them."

"You will ride with me in my litter," decided Amotl, and he ordered his bearers to stop. Coyotl shyly took his seat at one end, being sure to leave enough room for Amotl to loll comfortably as he had before.

Amotl said nothing to the boy, as the miles slipped away behind them—miles of dark golden-tan plain, touched with the blue spots of maguey, rimmed in the distance with the purply-blue hills. Yet Coyotl was happy, and little by little he built a small castle of hope in his heart—hope that Amotl might keep him, after all.

But near sunset, the walls and house-tops of Azcapozalco came into view, and outside the city a detachment of Montezuma's soldiers came marching, pennants and banners flying in the breeze that lifts just as night falls. Along the walls the fires began to burn, and even the moon as it rose, seemed colored red like the war cloaks of the army.

The soldiers stopped Amotl's party, and asked for the leader.

"I am he," called Amotl, and he commanded his bearers to lower the litter so that he might descend.

"Are you Amotl the merchant?"

"Yes."

"The Emperor, Montezuma, awaits you in the city. Follow us."

"Shall I get out now?" asked Coyotl in a small voice.

"No," said Amotl, and laid his hand kindly on the boy's arm. "I want you to come with me."

So it was that Coyotl really saw Montezuma.

Montezuma was waiting for Amotl in the inner room of the central temple. The room was scantily furnished, but a little fire burned in a rock basin, and the benches were covered with thick and lovely feather robes.

Montezuma was dressed in his war clothes—quilted cotton vests and leggings, and a thick cloak. Around his head he had tied a cotton band of red. His gold and feathered helmet lay to one side—too heavy to wear indoors.

Amotl bowed deeply, but Montezuma raised him almost immediately. Coyotl remained on the floor, his forehead on the ground, and he was trembling with pride and with awe to be in the presence of the great emperor of the Aztecs.

"Let the boy rise," said a deep voice, and as Coyotl rose he looked into the dark, worried, but kind eyes of his King.

Amotl said, "You know all—the attack upon us—the treachery of the noble Huitl, who had evaded taxes, and who was a leader of rebellion...?"

"Yes."

"I have little else to tell you, except that preparations for war go fast. Huitl's fate must have frightened any others who swayed between loyalty and treachery. I think there is nothing to fear until you reach the border."

"We will conquer at the border," said Montezuma fiercely. "The gods have promised victory. They have promised that our alliance will hold, and that we will remain a sovereign state for many years to come. Until we shall be swept away forever… But that I shall not live to see."

Amotl spoke then.

"Majesty, I crave pardon for bringing into your presence my slave…"

"Your slave?"

"Yes. But he has done you services. It was he who escaped from the fighting and ran back to the post house with the message of your courier, and he who by sending help saved me and my men. And it was also he who discovered the proof of Huitl's treachery."

Montezuma looked hard into Coyotl's face.

"This boy is no slave. He is of good blood. And his deeds are good. Let him be free. I say that he is a slave no longer."

Coyotl fell on his knees and tried to stammer his thanks and his pride. And yet sobs rose in his throat and made talking difficult.

Montezuma put out his hand, took the boy by the arm, and drew him near. "Why this?" he asked kindly and wonderingly.

"Amotl is a great man," breathed Coyotl thickly. "I would like to serve him. But he meant to sell me anyway."

"I say you shall not serve any man but me," said Montezuma.

Here Amotl cleared his throat, and shifted his weight from foot to foot embarrassedly.

"The boy is young to go into war, sire."

"Ah. You are interested in him, then? Had you plans for him then, other than selling him?"

"I am a stern man, Majesty. I believe in discipline, and this boy had broken discipline twice at the temple school. That is why they gave him to me. I told him I would sell him, and I meant to keep my word. But I had arranged that a proxy buy him for me, and then free him. I am an old man now, and I do not wish to marry again. I would like a young son. I was going to adopt him."

Coyotl seized Amotl's hand and pressed it against his forehead.

"He is now free," said Montezuma. "And if you

'I Say That He Is A Slave No Longer.'

acknowledge him before me as your adopted son, it is enough. I am the law."

"Before you, I acknowledge this boy, and he shall be my son," said Amotl, and he raised the boy and clasped him fondly.

"I will be a good son," said Coyotl, and he meant it, for his heart was bursting with gratitude and pride and happiness.

www.ingramcontent.com/pod-product-compliance
Lightning Source LLC
Chambersburg PA
CBHW021338060726
47591CB00006B/2087